LIGHTNING BOLT BOOKS™

The Dragonfly's Journey

Benjamin Tunby

Lerner Publications ◆ Minneapolis

Lerner Publications Company
A division of Lerner Publishing Group, Inc.
241 First Avenue North
Minneapolis, MN 55401 USA

For reading levels and more information, look up this title at www.lernerbooks.com.

Library of Congress Cataloging-in-Publication Data

Names: Tunby, Benjamin, author.
Title: The dragonfly's journey / Benjamin Tunby.
Description: Minneapolis : Lerner Publications, 2018. | Series: Lightning bolt books. Amazing migrators | Includes bibliographical references and index. | Audience: Ages 6 to 9. | Audience: Grades K to 3.
Identifiers: LCCN 2017019796 (print) | LCCN 2017045309 (ebook) | ISBN 9781512498103 (eb pdf) | ISBN 9781512486360 (lb : alk. paper) | ISBN 9781541511811 (pb : alk. paper)
Subjects: LCSH: Dragonflies—Juvenile literature. | Dragonflies—Migration—Juvenile literature.
Classification: LCC QL520 (ebook) | LCC QL520 .T86 2018 (print) | DDC 595.7/33—dc23

LC record available at https://lccn.loc.gov/2017019796

Manufactured in the United States of America
4-51595-33200-4/2/2025

Table of Contents

Meet the Dragonfly

A dragonfly flies above a wetland. This insect is a migrator. Migrators move from one area to another at different times of the year.

Some dragonflies migrate, and others do not.

A dragonfly's body has three parts. It has a head at the front of its body and a thorax in the middle. A dragonfly's back end is called the abdomen.

A dragonfly lands to rest. It uses its two eyes to look for something to eat. A dragonfly's eyes are made up of about thirty thousand small lenses.

The dragonfly's many lenses help it see more colors and details than humans can see!

A dragonfly eats other insects. Sometimes it will even eat smaller dragonflies. When it spots something, its four wings help it fly quickly to catch food.

A Dragonfly Hatches

Male dragonflies fight, race one another, and show their bright colors. They are trying to get the attention of a female.

A male and female dragonfly mate. Then the female lays eggs on a plant near water. Sometimes the male will stay with the female while she lays eggs.

In two to five weeks, the eggs hatch into nymphs. Nymphs look like small dragonflies without wings. Dragonflies live most of their lives as nymphs.

It takes three to five months for many migrating dragonflies to grow into adults.

A Dragonfly Migrates

An adult dragonfly has wings. The dragonfly can now fly long distances. It is ready to migrate.

Sometimes dragonflies travel in big groups when they migrate.

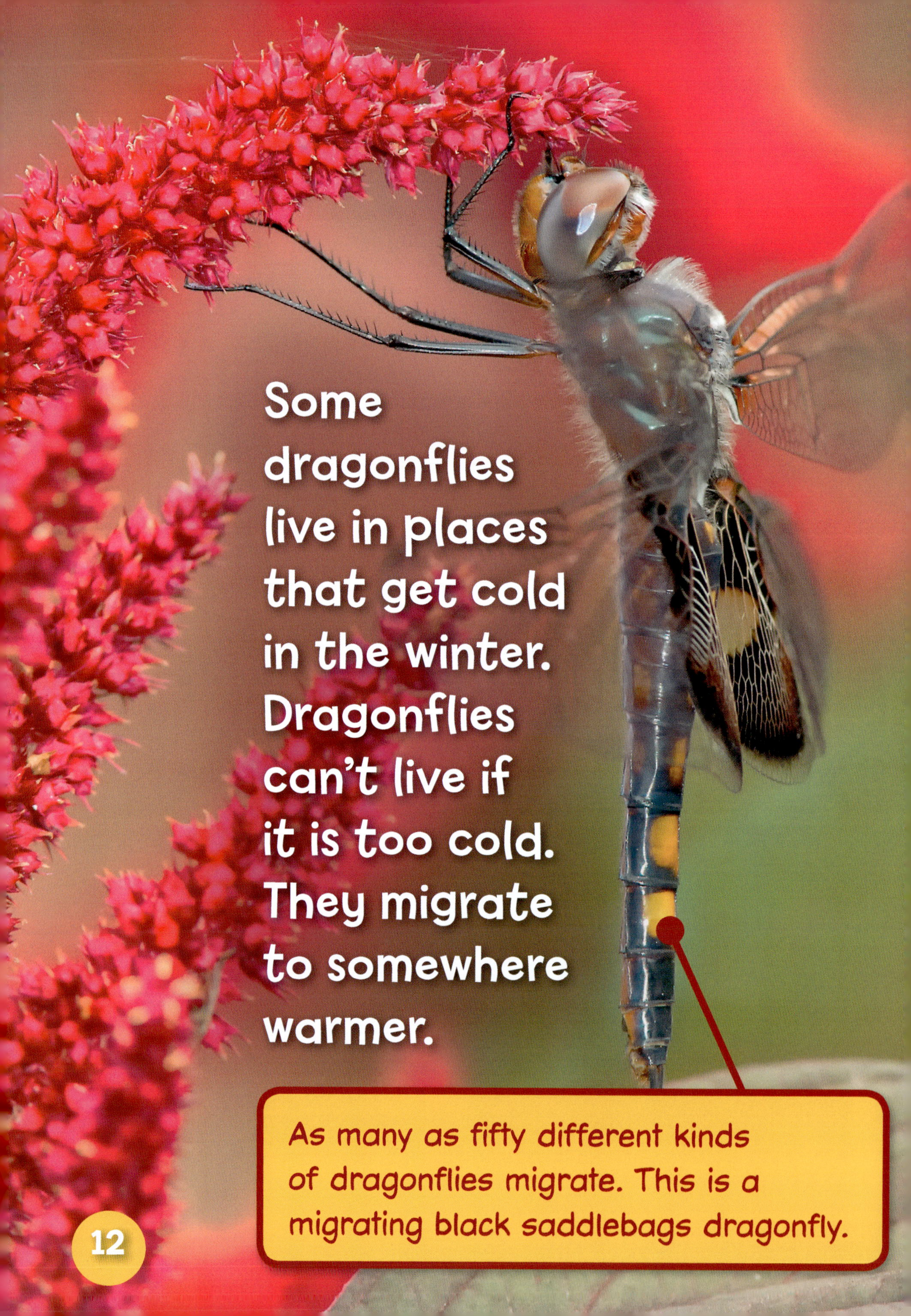

Some dragonflies live in places that get cold in the winter. Dragonflies can't live if it is too cold. They migrate to somewhere warmer.

As many as fifty different kinds of dragonflies migrate. This is a migrating black saddlebags dragonfly.

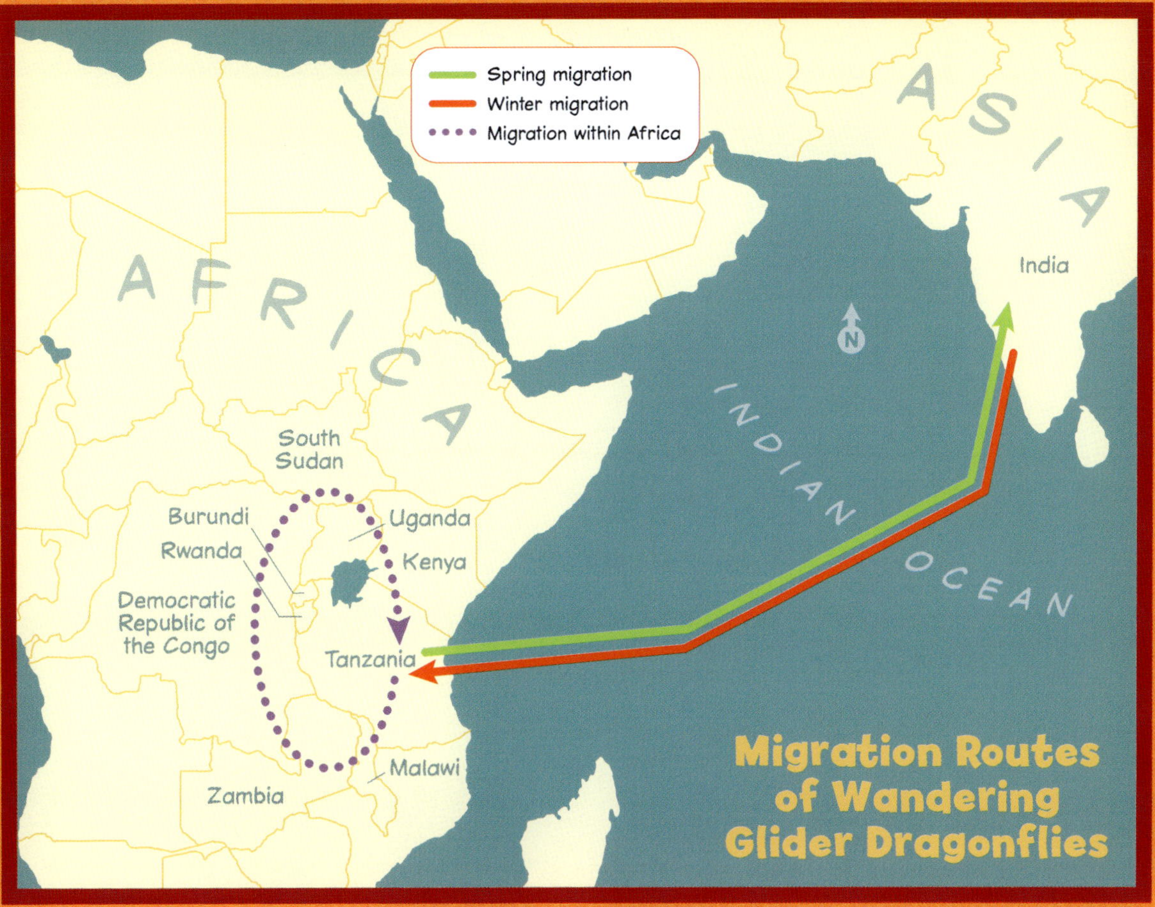

Migration Routes of Wandering Glider Dragonflies

The wandering glider dragonfly migrates farther than any other dragonfly. Its journey is from southern Asia to eastern Africa. It travels up to 11,000 miles (17,700 km) each year!

Common green darner dragonflies also migrate. They lay eggs during their long trip. Then the adult dragonflies die. The eggs hatch, and new dragonflies finish the migration north.

Migrating dragonflies return north when winter is over. They find water for their eggs.

This meadowhawk dragonfly has just returned from its migration.

Dragonflies in Danger

Dragonflies have many predators. They are eaten by birds, frogs, spiders, and larger dragonflies.

Dragonflies can see up, down, forward, and to the sides all at the same time.

But dragonflies escape from many predators. Their special eyes help them see predators all around them.

The biggest danger to dragonflies is people. People drain wetlands to make roads and buildings. This destroys the areas where dragonflies live.

But many people are trying to protect wetlands. Making new wetlands can also save dragonflies and other animals. Plans like these will help make sure that dragonflies will stay around for years to come.

Fun Facts

- Dragonflies live on every continent except Antarctica.
- Some dragonflies stay in cold waters during winter. They stay under a layer of ice as nymphs.
- The giant Hawaiian dragonfly is also called a *pinao*. This dragonfly can have a wingspan of up to 7.5 inches (19 cm).

More Amazing Migrators

- The desert locust is a kind of grasshopper. A migrating group of desert locusts can have more than a billion locusts!
- The convergent ladybug migrates twice a year. In California, thousands of these insects migrate to the mountains between May and June.
- The bogong moth lives in Australia. These moths migrate to mate in warmer parts of Australia because their young can't live in the cold.

Glossary

abdomen: a long, thin body part behind the thorax of a dragonfly

lens: a part of the eye that takes in light

mate: to join together to produce young

migrator: an animal that moves from one area to another at different times of the year

nymph: a young dragonfly that hasn't yet grown wings

predator: an animal that eats other animals

thorax: the middle body part of a dragonfly

wetland: an area of land that has a lot of water, including swamps, marshes, and bogs

Further Reading

All Things Animal TV: Dragonfly
https://m.youtube.com/watch?v=q5-KoPvZDlU

Bodden, Valerie. *Dragonflies*. Mankato, MN: Creative Education, 2013.

Cool Kid Facts: Dragonfly Facts
http://www.coolkidfacts.com/dragonfly-facts-for-kids

Ducksters: Dragonfly
http://www.ducksters.com/animals/dragonfly.php

Fishman, Jon M. *The Monarch Butterfly's Journey*. Minneapolis: Lerner Publications, 2018.

Stewart, Melissa. *Zoom In on Dragonflies*. Berkeley Heights, NJ: Enslow, 2014.

Index

Photo Acknowledgments

The images in this book are used with the permission of: Anthony Hall/Shutterstock.com, p. 2; BergelmLicht/Shutterstock.com, p. 4; Brian Lasenby/Shutterstock.com, pp. 5, 9; khlungcente/Shutterstock.com, p. 6; iStock.com/emprised, p. 7; ©Brooke Lewis/Dreamstime.com, p. 8; ©John Abbott/Minden Pictures, p. 10; blickwinkel/Alamy Stock Photo, p. 11; Paul Reeves Photography/Shutterstock.com, p. 12; ©Laura Westlund/Independent Picture Service, p. 13; ©Oakdalecat/Dreamstime.com, p. 14; Leia Hewitt/Alamy Stock Photo, p. 15; Dave Montreuil/Shutterstock.com, p. 16; John A. Anderson/Shutterstock.com, p. 17; Willowpix/E+/Getty Images, p. 18; Tiffany Bryant/Shutterstock.com, p. 19; Melinda Fawver/Shutterstock.com, p. 22.

Front cover: Vishnevskiy Vasily/Shutterstock.com.

Main body text set in Billy Infant regular 28/36. Typeface provided by SparkType.